CHOOSE YOUR OWN
ADVENTURER

ALI HOUSE

Distributed by:
Engen Books
www.engenbooks.com
submissions@engenbooks.com

First mass market paperback printing: March 2021

Cover Design: Ali House

CHOOSE YOUR OWN ADVENTURER

CAMPAIGN 2
THE CAVE OF SOULS

TABLE OF CONTENTS

THE GOBLIN CAVE

Grendel released a fierce yell as he brought his axe down, felling the goblin in front of him. He quickly fixed his gaze on another opponent – which wasn't difficult to find in the goblin-infested cave. Pretending that the small green creature coming for him was a certain not-to-be-named warlock, he raised his axe and let out another battle-cry.

As the axe came down, a bright yellow flash whizzed past Grendel's eyes, missing him by mere inches. He looked in the direction the flash had come from and glared. The slim young man who'd cast the lighting strike let out a hurried "Sorry!" before turning his attention back to the two goblins attacking him. Growling, Grendel turned away from Corin and look-ed for another opponent to slash at.

Corin shrieked as one of the goblins in front of him

lunged forward. In its hands was a rudimentary spear, but the end looked sharp enough to do real damage and Corin quickly brought up his right hand and cast a shield to protect himself. The spear bounced off the translucent blue oval that appeared, but the goblin was not deterred.

Taking a step back, Corin wondered if he should call out for help. He was definitely in over his head. With two opponents attacking at once, he was too busy defending himself to properly fight, and any spells he managed to cast usually went wild. However, he wasn't sure calling for help would make any difference. Aeris had been backed into a corner by a mob of goblins and was trying her best to dispatch them, Rev was nowhere to be seen and had probably left them all to die, and Grendel seemed to have no desire to help, despite having had plenty of opportunities to do so. Corin wasn't sure what would be worse – having Grendel resent him for having to leap in and save him or having Grendel blatantly ignore him. He knew which outcome would be more likely.

The second goblin interrupted his thoughts by slashing at him with a rock that had been fashioned into a dagger, and Corin brought the shield around, managing to block the attack. His heart was racing, his blood was pumping, and he was almost certain he was going to die here. Why did he ever think he could be an adventurer? He should have gone to a small village and found a small shack and made a small life for himself, but instead he was going to die in a cave, murdered by goblins, while everyone else made more money by splitting their fee three ways instead of four.

Pushing down the panic that was rising within,

Corin used his left hand to aim a spell at the goblin holding the spear, hitting it in the chest with an invisible stone and knocking it to the floor. His triumph was short-lived as another goblin broke away from the group around Grendel and hurried over, spear raised above its head. When the goblin on the floor picked up its own fallen spear and got back on its feet, Corin felt all hope drain from his body.

Aeris swung her sword in a wide arc, cutting down one goblin and pushing the rest of them back. She couldn't help being disappointed in herself for not insisting that they check out the cave before rushing in. Sure, Rev hadn't wanted to go into the cave alone, and Grendel was insistent that there couldn't be more than eight goblins inside, and Corin hadn't given an opinion either way, but she should have overruled them all. And now, because she'd let them have their way and hadn't demanded they listen to her, they'd run straight into a cave of thirty murderous goblins.

They'd had a plan, of course, but it was a plan for defeating only eight goblins, so it had fallen apart within seconds of their arrival.

Swinging her sword again, she noticed that Corin was now facing three goblins and that there was a look of panic on his face. Frustration welled up inside of her, but she pushed it down. She needed to get rid of the pile of goblins surrounding her, then help Corin, then help Grendel, and then figure out where the heck Rev had run off to. The only problem was that she was having trouble focusing on one task at a time. How could she concentrate on the goblins in front of her when Corin was obviously struggling to stay alive?

Looking over at Grendel, she saw that he was also

fighting a group of goblins and was cutting through them viciously. Unfortunately, he wasn't being careful with his attacks and a move that might have brought down an enemy was only injuring it. He could have finished this fight in a few minutes if only he'd pay more attention. And where was Rev? Why wasn't she helping them? She had weapons, so why wasn't she using them? Couldn't she see how desperate the situation was?

A goblin lunged for her and Aeris barely stepped to the side in enough time to avoid the attack. Bringing her sword down, she dispatched the goblin and tried to focus on the rest of the group.

How had this simple task become such a mess? She was about to chide herself for past mistakes, but then she had a sudden epiphany that thinking on the past was useless. She needed to think about the future. Focus on the first task – which was cutting through these goblins – and hopefully Corin would be able to hold out for a few more minutes until she could help him.

Her determination restored, Aeris attacked the goblin closest to her, taking it down with one swing of her sword. Now that her head was clear and she wasn't trying to solve every problem at once, she was able to focus on attacking quickly and efficiently.

After a few minutes and some careful attacks, she'd managed to take down all of the goblins around her. A quick glance at Grendel told her that he could handle himself for a while longer, so she rushed over to Corin. He still had the shield up, but his left hand was pressed tightly to his side and it looked liked he was losing steam. She moved her focus to the three goblins crowding him. Two of them immediately turned towards her, glaring at the new threat. Summoning what remained of her strength, she waited until they were within striking distance before swinging her longsword in a wide arc.

Once those two were dispatched, she quickly took down the remaining goblin, who had been desperately trying to get his makeshift dagger past Corin's shield. Corin didn't say anything, but gave her a look of infinite appreciation, his eyes wide and his face pale.

She nodded at him before looking back at Grendel, who had two goblins left. He looked like he had things in hand and, to be perfectly honest, she was afraid of getting in the path of his battleaxe, so she remained with Corin.

"Are you okay?" she asked.

"Just a quite painful scratch," he replied with a forced smile. His hand remained pressed to his side.

"But are you going to survive the next five minutes?" she clarified.

He nodded.

Aeris glanced around for Rev, but still couldn't see the shorter woman. Although there were two camp-fires burning inside the cave, tossing flickering light across the ground and rough walls, there were plenty of shadows for her to blend into, or plenty of time for her to have run away. Aeris wondered again why she'd agreed to work with a rogue. Although Rev had proven to be quite helpful in their fight against the evil warlock Grimgrax, Aeris knew that most rogues only cared for themselves. Perhaps it had only been a matter of time before Rev showed her true colours.

This job was supposed to be a chance for the four

of them to prove that their last victory hadn't been pure luck, and that maybe they could work together as a team, solving problems all across the land. Obviously, it wasn't working out the way she'd thought. Maybe after this job was over she should head off and continue her quest to complete enough trials to become a high-level paladin on her own.

"Ha!" Grendel cried as he vanquished his last foe. Resting his axe on the ground, he wiped the sweat from his brow and looked around the cave. "Is that all?"

Aeris had a few things she wanted to say to that remark, but she diplomatically held her tongue.

"Where's Rev?" Corin asked. "We didn't injure her by mistake, did we?"

"You wish," the dark-haired woman said as she moved out of the shadows near the back of the cave.

Again, Aeris held back what she actually wanted to say. Those sort of words wouldn't be becoming of a paladin-in-training. "I guess the job's finished," she remarked instead, looking around the cave. The farmer they'd talked to back at The Last Chapter tavern had never seen more than eight goblins attack his fields at once, but apparently this nest liked to divide and conquer. She wondered how many other farms in the area had been suffering from goblin attacks. Perhaps this deed had helped more than one person.

Grendel gestured to the piles of objects scattered throughout the cave. "Do you think there's anything of interest in there?"

Rev laughed bitterly. "It's nothing but vegetables and rudimentary weapons." Suddenly she noticed that the other three were staring at her, their eyes narrow and faces serious. "What?" she asked.

Aeris paused, a deep frown crossing her face. "Were you looting the cave while we were fighting for our lives?"

"...No." Rev crossed her arms over her chest. "It was really crowded in here and I was worried that if I did anything I might hurt one of you. So I stayed out of the way, okay?"

Sighing, Aeris decided not to pursue the matter any further and moved over to the nearest pile. "We might as well take some of these things with us. Maybe Walton can salvage some of the vegetables, if they're not too rotten. It may not be diamonds, but the goblins stole from him, so he deserves something back."

"Um..." Corin said before falling silent again, his gaze dropping to the floor.

"Oh, right!" Aeris quickly turned back to him. "Let's get you closer to the fire and I'll see what I can do."

With Aeris' help, he moved over to the nearest fire and took his hand off the wound. It was deeper than she'd expected, but it hadn't bled too much thanks to the pressure he'd kept on it. She took in a deep breath and placed her hands over the wound. Calling on Arete, she prayed for the ability to heal Corin's wound and make him well once again. She felt a surge of holy power fill her and exit through her hands. When she looked at Corin's wound she saw that the skin had managed to knit itself back together and was no longer bleeding. "Remember to take it easy for the next few hours," she instructed him. "I'm still an apprentice, after all."

When she turned back to the others, she saw that

Rev and Grendel were standing there, watching her.

"Do either of you need healing?" she asked politely, knowing full well that Rev had hidden from all danger and that Grendel wouldn't accept any help unless his life depended on it. Both of them shook their heads. "Then don't you have vegetables to gather?" she added, irritation creeping into her tone. They both nodded and each moved towards a pile.

"I'll help," Corin said, stepping away from the fire.

"No, you were injured, so you're allowed a bit of a rest. Besides, if you do too much you might end up ripping the wound open. I'll gather a few things for you to carry on the way back. *Light* things."

She turned away and walked over to one of the piles to search for any decent vegetables. After leaving paladin school, she had been prepared to wander the land, helping anyone who needed assistance and earning her place as a fully-fledged paladin, one experience at a time. She'd known that it would be a difficult path and fraught with many tests, but she'd never expected to end up in this kind of situation. Being part of a group had sounded fun, and she'd secretly hoped that she would be able to influence the others to be good and kind, but it was much more frustrating than she'd initially thought.

If this was all a test, hopefully it would count for a lot of experience.

THE TRIUMPHANT RETURN

There weren't many vegetables that could be salvaged – apparently goblins didn't care if the food they kept was fresh or not – but the group managed to gather four small bundles to take with them. The walk to Walton's farm wasn't long, but the group travelled in silence. Aeris was still annoyed and worried that she might say something she'd regret, Grendel was revelling in the high that came after a battle, Rev didn't want to call attention to herself, and Corin was afraid of saying the wrong thing and making everyone hate him.

"You're back!" Walton said cheerfully as he greeted them at the door. "Does that mean all of the goblins are gone?"

Aeris nodded and opened her mouth to speak, but Rev cut her off.

"They're all gone," Rev said. "Which was no small feat as that little nest turned out to contain about forty of them."

Walton's eyes widened. "Forty?"

"Yeah," Rev nodded. "So it was quite a daunting task."

"But one that we were definitely up to," Aeris quickly added. "Your farm should be safe from goblins for a while."

"Wow..." Walton gave a low whistle as he led the group into his kitchen. "I'd never have thought there'd be that many..."

"Perhaps your farm wasn't the only one being targeted," Aeris replied. She placed her small bundle on the table. "We managed to save a few vegetables, but there wasn't much."

Walton's eyes went wide again as the others also put their bundles down. "Well, this is more than I was expecting."

"Tell me about it," Rev quietly remarked, earning an elbow in the side from Aeris.

Aeris put on her best smile. "Well, you know what they say about plans..." The question was supposed to be rhetorical, but everyone turned to look at her and she found herself scrambling for some kind of an answer. "You... always need multiple?"

"Well, unfortunately I can't offer you any more money for your troubles," Walton said, "especially after those interfering goblins darn near ruined my crops, but if you return in a month or so, I can set some preserves aside for you."

Rev and Grendel fell silent, and Aeris could tell that they'd been hoping to get a few more coins out of this adventure.

"Well," Aeris said quickly, "we'll have to see where the adventuring road takes us, but that sounds good to me." She waited for the others to chime in, and when they didn't she cleared her throat loudly.

"Such a great offer," Corin quickly stammered.

"That'll be good enough," Rev said blandly.

"What she said," Grendel muttered.

Aeris forced a smile on her face. "I guess we can take our payment and then take our leave, sir."

Walton laughed. "You don't need to call me 'sir'. Just know that if I had treasure lying around, I'd surely give you all of it for helping me with my problem."

Aeris shot a look at Rev, warning her not to say anything. She was sure that the rogue would be kinder if there had been treasure in that cave, but since there had been nothing of worth, the shorter woman was trying to find gains any other way possible. Aeris needed to get payment from the farmer and get the group out of here before they said something to insult him. It was difficult enough to make a name for yourself in this world; they didn't need those they'd helped speaking ill of their behaviour. Once they'd left the farm, perhaps she could make her excuses and go on her merry way, free to adventure on her own, without anyone else interfering.

"Now wait a minute..." Walton trailed off, putting a finger to his lips. "Treasure..."

Everyone perked up and held their breath as they waited for him to finish his train of thought.

"Now, my old buddy Dillen heard something about a treasure hidden in a cave somewhere in these parts. I though it was a tall tale, to be honest, but seeing as how you're all the adventuring type, maybe it's be something you'd like to look into."

"You're right about that," Rev said. "Where's this Dillen? Where can we find him?"

"Well, it's a bit late, but he's always up for a drink and a story. I could send Lukas to fetch him. Probably have him here in twenty minutes."

The concept of treasure was highly enticing, but Aeris wasn't sure if she wanted to go bothering locals to hear tall tales of treasures that may or may not exist. However, she didn't have any chance to offer an opinion before Rev was on the case.

"That sounds great!" Rev exclaimed. "I'd love to hear that story. Tell Lukas to hurry."

"I'll go get him right away," Walton smiled. "Then, when I come back, I'll bring your pay and pour you all a drink."

Walton hurried out of the kitchen, eager to fetch his farmhand. Once he was gone, Aeris turned to Rev.

"What are you doing?" she said quietly. "We don't have time for this."

"What else are we doing?" Grendel interjected. "Besides, I like the idea of getting a drink or two out of this."

Rev gave Aeris a knowing look. "Legends have to start somewhere. I know that it's possible this cave isn't full of treasure, or maybe doesn't even exist, but if there's a chance that I can get some sweet coin across my palm, I want to take it."

Aeris frowned. "What if some of us don't want to do this?" she asked.

Rev looked around the room. Grendel crossed his arms and nodded at her; Corin looked around nervously before shrugging his shoulders. She turned back to the paladin. "Do you not want to do this?"

"Well, I mean, I'm supposed to be helping people, not adventuring for monetary gains," Aeris said, struggling with her words. She knew that she should come right out and speak of her intentions to leave the group, but didn't think that this would be a good place to do so.

Rev paused and considered the situation. "How about you help us get this treasure and then you donate your portion to us? That would be pretty helpful and selfless."

"Sounds good to me," Grendel chimed in.

Aeris felt her frustration rise to the surface. "Yeah, well what if we don't get the treasure, because when we go inside this cave we all do our own thing again and get killed? Do you know how close we came to dying because of a nest of goblins?"

"It wasn't that bad," Rev said, waving her hand noncommittally.

"It was three times what we were expecting! Grendel raced in, forgetting that the rest of us were there within seconds; Corin got separated and cornered almost instantly; and you were no help at all! If this cave is supposed to be truly dangerous, then we could all die!"

Grendel frowned. "Speak for yourself. I was handling things just fine."

Corin pressed his lips together and hunched his shoulders, as if trying to disappear.

"Okay," Rev conceded, "that fight didn't go as smoothly as we'd have liked it to. But who's to say the next one won't be better? I mean, we're the heroes that defeated Grimgrax! We should be able to handle a cave of treasures."

Aeris felt as if her point had been diverted from its true course. Rev and Grendel were determined and she doubted that she could say anything to stop them. She turned to Corin. "Are you sure you want to do this?"

Corin paused and licked his lips. "I will confess that during the goblin fight there was a moment where I wished that I was safe at home with a nice cup of tea. However, I do not have enough money to buy or build a home, so I would have to settle for being safe in a bush or under a tree. It would be nice to have enough money to settle down..."

And with that, her last bargaining chip was gone. Aeris knew that she could walk away and wash her hands of the three of them, but deep down she suspected that they'd all die without her. It wasn't a conceited thought – it was based on fact and past experiences. And although she was annoyed with each of them, she didn't wish them dead.

Gazing up at the roof of the house, she said a quick prayer to Arete, hoping that the god was watching her and noticing this good deed she was about to do.

"Fine," she sighed. "We'll listen to Dillen's tale, and if it seems plausible, we'll seek out the cave. But I want us to promise that we'll try to work as a team this time."

The other three nodded solemnly. She wasn't convinced.

†

Despite the late hour, Dillen arrived with bright

eyes and bountiful energy. He bounded into Walton's home, greeting everyone cheerfully before setting up near the hearth, hand held out for the expected mug of ale.

"Did Lukas fill you in on what we're looking for?" Walton asked as he handed Dillen his drink.

Dillen took a large swig. "Yup. Told me you're all lookin' to hear about the Cave of Souls." He smiled and motioned for them all to gather 'round. Rev sat on the floor in front of him, eager to hear the tale, while the others found chairs and boxes to settle upon. Once they were all seated, Dillen gave a hearty laugh and began to weave a tale...

Once upon a time there was a young man who was studying to become a wizard. He lived in a remote village and did not have the money to travel or hire a tutor, so he studied on his own. Within his village was a small library, but it included many journals from a wizard who had been slain nearby, so the young man used these to study and become powerful.

He learned many things, and not all of them were nice. But he was hungry for knowledge and desired to know everything – good or bad.

There was only one thing that could distract him from his work. At the library worked a young woman, and although she was equally nice with all the other patrons, after a while he became infatuated with her. She never returned his feelings and would politely turn him down whenever he asked her to join him for a walk or a meal, but it did not deter him. He convinced himself that if only he could become the greatest wizard in the land, then she would love him.

Over time, he learned many great spells, and although most could be used for protection, he realized that they could also be twisted for darker purposes. As he manipulated these spells, so too did his own mind become twisted; and as the young man's power grew, so did the feeling that he had earned the young woman's attention.

One night, he ambushed the young woman in her home and demanded that she become his forever. She refused and the wizard killed her instantly. However, before her spirit could ascend into the otherlands, the wizard encased it in a crystal. Then he stole away, to a hidden cave, and placed the crystal inside. He told the soul that he would leave her here, all alone, and that one day he would come back and ask her that question again. Hopefully this time her answer would be different.

He placed many protections around the cave to keep the crystal safe from anyone who might wander inside. Outside, he marked the entrance with a sigil, so that he would always be able to find it.

But when he returned home, the villagers were waiting for him. Word had spread about the young woman's murder, and they quickly grabbed him and strung him up, tying him to a prepared pyre. As he began to burn, he cried out, "Her soul's in the cave!"

They demanded answers, but as the flames grew, he refused to speak any more. And then he died.

The villagers searched high and low for the cave, hoping to free the young woman's soul, but they never found it. To this day, her soul remains in the crystal, waiting to be rescued.

"They say that the cave is located in the Mwsogl Mountains, near the Eastern waterfall. The sigil is supposed to be carved into the rock next to the waterfall, just a few feet from the entrance." Dillen paused to finish his drink. "Others have tried to go in, but most never return. The few who have speak of skeletons and creatures and things worse than nightmares."

He fell silent and gestured to Walton to pour him another drink.

"What a terrible story," Aeris remarked, mostly to herself. "That poor woman."

"Hey," Rev spoke up. She'd listened attentively to the entire story, but now she had a confused look on her face. "You didn't mention anything about treasure."

Dillen laughed. "Oh yeah. They say the cave is where the wizard stored all of his treasures. You know, to keep them out of the hands of the other townsfolk."

"Sounds likely," Rev nodded. "But why's it called the Cave of Souls if there's only one soul in the crystal?"

He shrugged. "Why do we call anything anything? It's just a name." He seemed satisfied by his answer, but Rev wasn't. She fell silent and stared off, lost in thought.

"The Mwsogl Mountains aren't far," Grendel said to the others. "They're less than two days walk from here."

"Corin, do you have a map?" Aeris asked.

Corin had been deep in thought, but snapped out of it at the mention of his name. "Oh, yeah. I do. Do we need it now?"

"We'll look at it later," Aeris said. "I think it's time

to take our leave and head back to the tavern."

She looked at the others, but nobody disagreed with her.

"Thank you for your story, Dillen," she said. "And thank you, Walton, for letting us stay to hear it. We wish you the best in your farming endeavours."

"Ah," Walton replied, brushing off the compliment, "y'all did me a big favour there. I wish you the best if you decide to check out this cave."

They said their goodbyes and then the group headed back to The Last Chapter to fetch some rooms for the night.

"I wonder why it's called the Cave of Souls if there's only one soul in it..." Rev mused out loud as they walked. "Do you think there might be other people trapped in crystals in there? The wizard's enemies perhaps?"

Corin looked horrified by the suggestion. "I hope not," he said quietly.

Rev frowned. "I wonder..."

They walked for a few more minutes in silence before Grendel spoke up.

"We're definitely doing this, right?" he asked. "I mean, I could kill some creatures for a bit of treasure."

"Of course we are," Rev replied immediately. "I mean, with a tale like that, how could we not check it out?" She looked over at Aeris. "Right?"

Aeris nodded, all of her reluctance gone. After that tale, she knew that she had to go to this cave and set that young woman's soul free. "We'll meet up at breakfast to plan our route and then head out towards the mountains."

She looked over at Corin, who was frowning to

himself, but when he noticed her looking at him, he nodded emphatically, forcing a smile onto his face. Aeris detected that he was acting stranger than usual, but wasn't sure why. Perhaps the story had frightened him.

"For now," she said, "let's get back to the tavern and get some sleep. It might be the best night's rest we have for a few days."

THE PLAN

The group met for breakfast early the next morning, and all were eager to start planning their journey to the Mwsogl Mountains – even Corin. The night's rest seemed to have reinvigorated him and he was now approaching the task with a quiet determination.

They dined on meat and bread, drinking their morning brew as they examined the map that Corin had brought. The only sound in the air was chewing as their eyes traced over the parchment. However, it wasn't long before trouble reared its ugly head.

"We should take the Western road," Aeris started, following the path with her finger. "It's the most direct route and will get us there by early-afternoon tomorrow."

"No," Grendel argued almost immediately. "If we

cut through the forest, then we'll shave hours off the journey."

"That may be true, but the journey will still take longer than a day. If we follow the road we'll be able to find a tavern for the night."

"Tavern?" he scoffed. "We have bedrolls. Could save us a bit of money, sleeping under the stars."

Rev nodded. "We don't know how many other people know about this cave. We should get there as fast as possible, otherwise they might get all the treasure."

"But the cave's going to have monsters inside," Corin said cautiously. "Maybe we should take the easier route and save our strength until we get there."

Grendel rolled his eyes and bit into a piece of meat. "You need to stop being so scared of everything," he said, his words barely intelligible around his full mouth.

"It's not fear!" Corin quickly defended. "I'm trying to be strategic." Despite his attempt to stand up to Grendel, his posture reflected differently as his shoulders began to draw inward.

"We should take the road," Aeris said firmly. "We don't know what kind of things are in those woods, and we shouldn't be taking unnecessary risks. Especially when we're expecting to walk into a cave full of unknown threats."

Rev frowned. "There's nothing in those woods, Aeris. Maybe a few animals, but those'll be easy enough to deal with. I say we go for it."

Corin looked at Aeris, concerned, and she knew that he was hoping she'd make a final decision. The problem was that it wouldn't be easy. The group was split right down the middle – half of them wanting to take the road and the other half wanting to go through the forest. It would be easy if it was three versus one, but that wasn't the case here.

Aeris tried to think of what would be best. As much as she'd like to take a few hours off the journey, she suspected that travelling through the woods wouldn't be so easy. The path wouldn't be as well-trod as a road, and what if they ran into a bear or wolves? But she had a feeling that neither Rev nor Grendel would budge.

"How about we split up?" she said.

Everyone looked at her, confused.

"We know that our best bet for conquering the cave is for us all to be together, but we're never going to agree on a route. So let's split up and meet at the waterfall, and once we're together again, we can go in." She smiled, satisfied with her solution, and took a sip of her drink.

"But that's going to defeat the purpose of shaving a few hours off our journey," Rev pointed out. "Are Grendel and I going to have to sit down and stare at the waterfall while we wait for you two to finally arrive?"

"You can search for the sigil, to confirm that we have the right spot," Aeris said helpfully.

"That'll take a whole minute," Grendel muttered before taking another fierce bite.

Aeris sipped her drink again. "Well, I happen to think that we won't be so far behind you. The forest is full of strange creatures, and if you have to stop and fight them, we'll have time to catch up."

A smile broke out on Rev's face. "Oh... You wanna

race."

Aeris was confused. "What?" She looked over at Corin, who shrugged.

"Well then," Rev continued, nodding, "we'll have a race. Winning team gets first pick of the treasure!"

Aeris opened her mouth to argue, but then realized that this might be exactly what she needed. "Yes, let's race," she smiled.

Rev's smile widened and she turned to Grendel. "In that case, let's get going!" The two of them started grabbing food, working so swiftly that Aeris had to wonder if they'd discussed this possibility the night before. When their pockets were full, they grabbed their things and hurried out the door.

"Um... Should we follow them?" Corin asked.

Aeris shook her head. "Let's at least finish our breakfast. They'll be stumbling over fallen logs and dodging branches while we'll have a nice well-worn path to walk." Smiling to herself, she picked up a piece of bread and took a triumphant bite.

†

To follow Aeris and Corin's Path, continue forward.

Or you can follow to Grendel and Rev's Path
on Page 39.

Or you can skip over the journey
and head straight to The Cave of Souls on Page 55.

AERIS AND CORIN'S PATH

Despite Aeris saying that there was no need to rush, the two of them didn't dawdle in the tavern for long and were soon on the Western road. Neither cared about arriving first – although both admitted to themselves that it would be satisfying – but they didn't want to risk arriving too long after the others. That would be the kind of thing Rev would never let them live down.

At first the walk was uneventful. The sun was shining, a few wispy clouds were in the bright blue sky, the wind was mild, and it looked like a great day for travel. They were making good time along the road, but less than an hour after they'd started out, they ran into trouble.

"Thief! Stop! Thief!"

Both of them paused at the words, even though

they knew that neither of them were thieves and that Rev had to be far, far away by now. Exchanging a look, they hurried down the road, towards the cry. Around a bend, they noticed a figure standing on the path, waving his arms and frantically calling for help.

Aeris sped up, running towards the figure. When she reached the man she quickly skidded to a stop. "What's the problem?" she asked.

"There was someone on the road," the man said, eyes wide with shock at her sudden appearance. "He asked for help, but then pulled a knife and took all I had."

"Where'd he go?"

The man pointed into the woods and Aeris nodded. With a glance behind her, to make sure that Corin was following, she took off into the trees.

The path the thief had run off in was easy enough to follow. There were plenty of broken branches and the ground was trampled. After a few seconds of running, she was able to make out the thief in the distance. He turned around and, upon noticing her, sped up. Aeris narrowed her eyes and continued the chase.

Less than a minute later, she'd caught up to him, tackling him to the ground. Jumping to her feet, she pulled out her longsword and held it towards the thief. "I demand you return what you have taken and that you come with me to the authorities!"

The man's eyes widened as the blade came close to his throat. "I... I'm sorry. I needed the money to... feed... my family."

"And I am sure the man you stole this money from also has mouths to feed," she replied, keeping her sword steady. She was quite certain that the thief was lying, but didn't want to call him a liar without proof. "There are better ways to earn money than by taking it from someone else."

Corin burst through the woods, quickly coming to a stop as he noticed that she had everything in control. He looked over at her and she gave a nod to him before turning her attention back to the thief.

"March," she ordered, and the thief cautiously rose to his feet. Corin led the way back to the road and the thief followed. Aeris brought up the rear, her sword ready.

It was slower getting back to the road, but Aeris didn't want to give the thief a chance to get away. The man who'd been robbed was still where she'd left him, and considering how wide his eyes went at their return, he'd likely expected them to come back empty-handed.

"Return what you have stolen from this man," Aeris commanded.

The thief grumbled, but obediently returned a small bag of coins to the man.

"How far are we from the nearest town?" she asked the man.

"Oh, you're only a few minutes away from Greenvale," he replied, pointing in the direction Corin and she had been heading before all of this. "I was just starting out for Humville when this happened."

Aeris bowed her head. "Thank you, sir. I'll be sure to bring this thief to the authorities. You can return to your journey."

The man thanked them and nodded before heading off, walking at a brisk pace.

Sighing, Aeris told the thief to start marching again and not get any ideas of running.

The three of them received a few strange looks as they entered Greenvale, but when she asked for directions to the local guard station, the people caught on immediately. Someone pointed the way, and the odd group continued through town.

The guards were surprised to see the man be marched into their building, but also thankful. The man was a known thief, and they'd received word not long ago about him having been seen around these parts, so were thankful to have him apprehended.

After their good deed was done, Aeris and Corin headed back to the road, but their exit was quickly disturbed by frantic shouts.

"Fire! Fire!"

Corin paused, nervously biting his lower lip. "We're going to help, aren't we?"

Aeris nodded. She knew that he was more nervous about losing time than fighting a fire, and she'd be lying if she said the same thought hadn't crossed her mind. But she was a paladin, no matter how low-skilled, and she had to help.

They both hurried in the direction of the shouting, finding a small one-storey house that was partially ablaze. There were townsfolk rushing to and from the well, bringing empty buckets to be filled with water and transporting full buckets to be thrown on the fire, but they weren't able to combat the blaze. The flames were concentrated in the front room, with smoke billowing out of the open windows and doors, but it was high enough that the roof could catch at any minute.

"You don't happen to have any water spells, do you?" she asked Corin.

He shook his head. "I have some frost spells that I could try. It might not work as well, but it could help a bit."

"Then you'd better try. Cast it on the roof. If that goes up, we might lose the whole house."

Corin took in a deep breath and concentrated. Muttering a few words under his breath, he focused on the roof and cast Enver's Frost. The house was small enough that the entire roof soon became covered with a sheen of ice crystals.

"I don't know how long it'll last," he said, "especially with the fire underneath."

"Well, then we'd better see about getting that blaze under control," Aeris replied, taking in the scene and trying to figure out the best way to help. She noticed that most of the people throwing water on the blaze were doing so from a distance, keeping back from the heat and flames. She apologized as she grabbed a full bucket from one of them and hurried closer to the house, getting as close as she dared before throwing it on the fire. Turning around, she hurried back and exchanged her empty bucket for a full one, apologizing to the startled villager as she did. When people noticed what she was doing, they started guiding most of the buckets her way, making it so that she didn't have to go as far. On one of her trips she noticed that Corin had joined the bucket brigade.

There were moments when it felt like the fire would never end, but eventually the flames were quenched. The ice on the roof had started to melt, but the resulting water kept the roof wet enough to avoid catching fire. Although the front room of the house was not in good shape, by the time the last ember was out, the house was still standing.

"Thank you for being here!" a middle-aged woman said. She turned to Corin. "Whatever you did to the roof was amazing!"

Corin blushed and stammered a few unintelligible words.

"Is this your house?" Aeris asked, taking the focus away from the startled wizard so that he could pull himself together.

The woman nodded. "I'll need to do some checks to see what needs to be fixed, but thankfully I won't be rebuilding from scratch, thanks to you two. Usually we lose at least the entire roof, if not the whole house." The woman smiled and shook her head. "Any chance you two are thinking of sticking around?"

"Unfortunately not. We're just passing through," Aeris answered.

"That's too bad. Now, I hope you don't mind me asking, but would you do a walk-through with me? You seem strong, and I'd hate to have something fall on my head."

Aeris hesitated. She wanted to get back on the road, but the woman had a good point. The fire might not have weakened the roof, but it could have weakened a wall or one of the support beams. She glanced at Corin, who had finally managed to pull himself together. He gave her a small nod.

"I guess we could spare some time for a walk-through," she replied, smiling at the woman.

Before going in, Aeris made sure that all three of them had buckets of water, in case there were any smoldering bits that might threaten to flare up again. She walked around the house with the woman at her side, while Corin followed behind, keeping an eye and ear out for any sounds of possible structure failure. The house was small, but it took a while to examine everything the fire had touched and test it to make sure it wouldn't fall down. Although nothing needed to be fixed immediately, Aeris recommended to the woman that she replace a few things sooner rather than later. The woman offered to make them tea to thank them, but Aeris gently declined the offer, saying that they needed to get back on the road.

They managed to make it out of Greenvale without any more incidents. As they walked, their pace quickened, both of them aware of how much time their good deeds had taken.

"Well, that was exciting," Corin remarked.

Aeris nodded. "I do hope that there isn't too much more of this along the way." If this was a sign of things to come, their one-and-a-half day trip might take a week.

"Agreed. I mean, I don't mind helping people, not at all, but I don't want Grendel and Rev to blame us for being late to the cave." He sighed heavily.

"I'm sure they're running up against obstacles, too," Aeris said reassuringly. "Travelling through the woods is rarely easy."

"I hope so," Corin replied, his voice so soft that it was barely noticeable.

They managed to get a few hours of walking in without anything happening, but soon they came upon someone with a broken wagon who needed help. Corin had a brief thought that if Rev were with them, she'd suggest ducking into the woods and sneaking past; and if Grendel were with them, he'd march on past, ignoring the situation. He knew that Aeris would definitely stop, and she was right to do so. As much as he didn't want to be blamed for holding up Grendel and Rev, he knew that a good person wouldn't be able to walk past a man who obviously needed help.

"Bit of trouble?" Aeris asked the man as they drew closer.

The man was guarded, but after giving the two of them a good looking-over, he seemed to realize that they didn't mean any harm.

"Broken wheel," he said. He pointed to the wagon, which had dipped on the bottom left side.

"Do you need any help?"

He gave her a flat look.

Aeris cleared her throat. "Would you like us to help you?" she asked, refining the question.

The man thought about it for a few seconds and shrugged.

Aeris held back a frown. It seemed like the man needed help, but also that he wasn't going to expressly ask for it. A shrug wasn't a no, but it also wasn't a yes. For all she knew, this man was having a wonderful time standing next to a broken wagon, and any attempts to help would ruin his day.

"Sir, if you would like our assistance, please say yes. Otherwise we will go on our way and cease to bother you." She felt very pleased with this line, as it left out any possible ambiguity.

The man paused to think, and she felt herself growing impatient over how much time this task was taking – and they hadn't even done anything yet.

Taking a breath, she calmed herself and looked over to see how Corin was doing. He turned to her, his eyes full of questions. One of them was likely: 'How long are we going to wait for this man to answer?'

Almost grudgingly, the man finally nodded, and Aeris motioned for Corin to follow her as she went over to take a look at the wheel. Immediately, she noticed that the felloe had cracked and split open. Upon closer inspection, she could see that the spokes were twisting and the shape of the wheel was starting to bend. Aeris wasn't sure how long it would last, but eventually the wheel would break entirely. It wasn't helped by the fact that it was propping up a wagon full of supplies.

Corin quietly confessed that he had no idea how to properly fix the wheel, so Aeris tried to think of what she could do to solve the problem. She could go to the nearest town to find someone to fix the wheel, but that would take hours, or longer. The man who owned the wagon seemed to have given up all hope, judging from his lack of interest, and it was possible that he'd simply stand here for the next few hours, doing nothing. The best option would be for her to find some supplies to patch up the wheel well enough for the wagon to make it to its destination, where it could be properly fixed.

While the man continued to stand silently next to his wagon, Aeris and Corin went into the forest to look for some materials to help strengthen the felloe. She wasn't entirely certain what would help, but after some time Corin and she managed to add some support to the wheel using branches and rope, and she hoped that their work would hold long enough for the man to make it to the nearest wheelwright. Normally she'd offer to accompanying him to the next town, just in case, but that would take far too many hours. If Corin and she took too long to get to the cave, Rev and Grendel would go inside by themselves, and if anything happened to the two of them, she'd never forgive herself for not being there to help.

When they finished, the man looked at their work, silently judging their attempt, and then continued on his way. After hearing him grunt something that Aeris pretended was a thank you, Corin and she took off towards the next village. Their original plan had been to stop and sleep at the village after this one, but they'd lost a lot of time helping people, and it'd be safer to stay here rather than risk being on the roads late at night.

After procuring rooms, the two of them swore to wake up early and get on the road after a very quick breakfast. Tomorrow they'd make up for the time they missed today.

†

Like all good plans, it started out fine enough. They headed out as the sun was still rising, walking briskly to make up for lost time. For a while it was a peaceful walk, with nobody else on the road, and the only sound being their own footsteps and the sound of birdsong. But as the sun continued its path along the sky and the rest of the world woke up, they soon discovered that peace was not to be found.

Aeris swore that she had never been along a busier road in her life. When she'd first started out on her paladin training, she would have given anything to be on a road like this – one stocked full of people who needed her help. In between rescuing kittens from trees, looking for lost objects in the weeds along the road, resolving disputes, and trying to explain direct-ions to people who really should not be travelling without a guide, there wasn't much opportunity to make up for lost time. Aeris hoped that Rev and Grendel were coming up against similar distractions, or that they'd at least wait for them. With the pace Corin and she were going, they wouldn't make it to the waterfall until mid-afternoon at the earliest.

"Do you think Rev and Grendel were right about going through the forest?" Corin asked as they hurried along the road.

She opened her mouth to disagree, but then thought better of it. "I think when they talked about the road being slower, they didn't consider these kinds of obsta-cles, and neither did I. Arete knows that I've never travelled such a busy road before. If we hadn't come across all those people, we'd still be on track."

He nodded. "Do you suppose it's likely they've run into obstacles and have been held up, too?"

"I'd be surprised if they haven't, but I can't imagine them running into as many as we have."

Corin was silent for a while. "If they arrive long before we do, should we tell them about all the people we had to help?"

"Probably not," Aeris replied. "They'll think we're making up stories to justify how long it took us to get there. Best to keep this all to ourselves."

He nodded again.

Finally they neared the path towards the Mwsogl

Mountains, and Aeris couldn't help feeling a wave of relief at being away from the general populace. Hopefully they wouldn't run into anyone needing help in the woods.

The path had been worn down enough that they didn't have to hack and slash at their surroundings, and the two of them picked up their pace even more. She was convince that Rev and Grendel had already arrived at the waterfall, and she hoped that they'd still be waiting for them. She also hoped that there'd be a chance to rest for a few seconds before going into the cave.

Finally they emerged from the woods into a small clearing, the most striking feature of which was a large waterfall cascading into a pool of water. The mountains surrounded half of the pool, and extended far to either side. They rose so high that the tops were tipped with white.

When Aeris looked at the large rocks around the edge of the pool she noticed two figures and breathed a sigh of relief. Slowing their pace, Corin and she walked over to where Rev and Grendel were sitting. The two of them seemed to be relaxing as they reclined on the rocks overlooking the water, but there was something about their posture that was slightly tense and stilted.

"Hope we didn't keep you waiting too long," Aeris said as she walked over to the waterfall.

Rev turned to her and waved her hand dismissively. "We're taking the time to enjoy the view. You know, relax before the big adventure."

"So I take it you two didn't come across any trouble on your path?" Corin asked.

Grendel and Rev exchanged a look.

†

To follow Grendel and Rev's Path, continue forward.

Or you can skip over the journey
and head straight to The Cave of Souls on Page 55

GRENDEL AND REV'S PATH

Rev munched on a piece of bread as she made her way through the forest. Grendel was leading the way, tromping a rough path while occasionally looking at the map in his hands to make sure they were on the right track. It was a copy of Corin's map, which Rev had created last night while everyone else was asleep. She didn't want to relying on Corin to tell them where they were going, so she'd decided to make her own map which she could consult on her own time. It had to be done in secret so that nobody would know she'd made a copy, as she didn't want everyone to start looking to her for directions instead. A person could miss a lot of fun opportunities if their nose was constantly stuck in a map. Right now, however, she knew that it was best to share the map with Grendel so that their journey through the woods would be a little easier. Sure, it might not have all of the fine details of Corin's, but it was good enough. After the group had decided to split up, she'd considered stealing Corin's map and leaving him with her copy, but she didn't want to get any blame for Corin and Aeris losing the race.

Their pace wasn't as fast as it would be on a well-groomed path, but Rev knew that they'd more than make up for it with the shorter route. As she thought of the cave, her palms started to itch with anticipation. She couldn't wait to get into the cave and get her hands on all that treasure! If the others were distracted by the trapped soul, maybe she'd be able to pocket a few items without them noticing. She knew that Aeris didn't approve of her 'scouting missions,' but Aeris and the others were used to living a modest life. Grendel grew up on a farm, Corin lived with a weird wizard, and Aeris' paladin training had to have been simple. Meanwhile, before her parents tossed her out and disowned her, Rev had been living with every luxury. So why shouldn't she take a little more, especially when she desperately missed the taste of fine food and drinks? The others couldn't miss what they'd never had.

Walking soon grew boring, especially since Grendel was more preoccupied with following the map instead of making small talk. Rev tried to find ways to keep herself interested in the journey, but the only things around were trees, trees, and more trees. Her only escape was when she tried to imagine the kind of treasures that could be found inside an evil wizard's lair. Was he the kind of wizard that hoarded money? Or did he have a collection of gemstones and metals used in potions? Or was he the kind of person who collected expensive items so that other people couldn't have them? Hopefully it'd be all three!

The hours passed in silence, which was only broken when Grendel stopped walking and let out a loud '*harrumph.*'

Rev, who had been lost in thought, didn't stop in time and crashed into his back. "What's going on?" she asked. "Why did you stop?

Grendel turned to her and pointed at the ground. He lifted up one of his feet before slowly bringing it back down to the ground, which made a squelching sound. "We're heading into swampland."

Rev looked down and noticed that the ground was indeed damper than before. "And?"

Grendel sighed. "The ground's been getting wetter as we walk, which means there's likely a swamp up ahead, and those things tend to go from 'a bit wet' to 'knee-deep in water' in the matter of one step. However, there's no swamp marked on the map, so I don't know where it begins or ends."

"So what do we do?"

"I hope the answer to that would be 'not walk into a swamp'," he said gruffly.

Rev took in a breath and reminded herself that Grendel wasn't exactly a master tactician. She was about to turn to Aeris to see if she had a plan, but remembered that the paladin wasn't with them. It was up to her to be the leader.

As much as she didn't want to veer off the path, the last thing she needed was to walk straight into a swamp. Not only would it soak her clothing, but it would be even tougher going and would slow them down significantly. It was entirely possible that there wasn't a swamp and that the damp ground was the result of run-off from a nearby river, but she didn't want to risk it.

But which way should they go? From what she could recall, Corin's map hadn't had any swamplands marked on it, merely a vague forested area. What if she decided to turn left and it continued into more swampland? But what if the swamp was to the right?

"Well?" Grendel asked impatiently.

She narrowed her eyes at him. "If you want a quicker answer, think of one yourself."

He huffed and headed to the right. Rev wondered if he was so impatient that he'd decided to risk it and walk into the swamp, but then he stopped. A thoughtful look crossed his face as he pushed his foot into the ground. Then he walked to the left, passing in front of Rev, and did the same thing.

"What are you…?"

He pointed to the right. "The ground's less wet here, so we should go this way." Then he started walking, not checking to see if she was following.

For a moment, Rev stayed where she was, too stunned to move. How had Grendel managed to figure out the best direction to go before she did? Had the answer actually been that simple all along? No, she convinced herself, it was because Grendel was used to working with the land and she wasn't. She was more accustomed to city streets and taverns, and not tromping through the deep dark woods. Shaking her head, she quickly took off after him.

✝

Grendel's path turned out to be less damp, but it also was more westerly than north-west. As Rev walked she wondered how much time this was adding on to their journey. Even worse, the further they walked into the woods, the harder it became to discern a path. It was lucky that she had Grendel in front of her, leading the way through the thick branches and bushes, but he did nothing to discourage the blackflies that were buzzing around them, eager for a bite. It wasn't long before she remembered that she didn't like traipsing through forests.

Eventually the ground became more solid and they were able to turn more northerly, having hopefully skirted around the swamp. Although they'd been walking for hours, Rev felt her adrenaline kick in as they passed by this obstacle. Dreams of coins and gemstones danced in her head as they pushed forward through the forest.

Those dreams were soon interrupted by a low growling sound in the distance. Rev looked up at Grendel, wondering if he'd found another obstacle in their way, but he was merely huffing to himself, not growling.

"Hold on," she said softly, coming to a stop. But Grendel didn't hear her and continued walking. She quickly caught up with him and put a hand on his shoulder. When he turned in surprise, she put a finger to her lips to indicate that he should be quiet, and he raised an eyebrow inquiringly.

She paused and listened, placing the low growling

to their left. From the same direction they could hear branches snapping and leaves crunching as something slowly moved their way. Rev and Grendel stood still as they listened to the noise that was too close for comfort, her hand wrapping around the hilt of her dagger as Grendel tightened his grip on his axe. They couldn't see what was making the noise, but they could see the bushes moving in the distance and hear the sounds getting closer and closer.

Rev looked up to Grendel, her eyes asking, *'What should we do?'*

He shrugged.

It would be smart to run away, but if they made any noise then they might attract the creature, and most creatures could run faster than humans. They could try being stealthy, but Rev knew that Grendel wouldn't succeed in not making noise. She also recognized that she'd have to be a really terrible person to run off and leave him to face this threat alone. Not that it was fair for her to stick around since she wasn't as good a fighter as he was...

As the growling grew louder, she left her dagger in its sheath and moved her hand over to her small crossbow. She tapped Grendel on the shoulder, held up her weapon, and pointed to a nearby tree that looked easy to climb. At first he was confused, but then he realized what she was saying. He nodded before turning back to the noise, his axe ready.

Rev scrambled up the tree as quickly and quietly as possible, and when she was about six feet from the ground, she settled herself on a sturdy branch and positioned her crossbow. It was difficult to see through the mess of branches in front of her and on the ground, but she could make out shapes moving closer to Grendel. She could also see glimpses of grey fur. Wolves.

Levelling her crossbow, she waited until the creatures moved closer. Taking aim, she fired at one of the shapes, hoping that her shot would scare one or most of them away. There was a yelping sound, letting her know that she'd hit one of them. Grendel crouched and prepared himself.

Two wolves burst into sight, their teeth bared as they snarled at their opponent. One of them lunged for Grendel, who was ready for it. Rev reloaded and aimed for the second wolf. She noticed that there was no crossbow bolt sticking out of it, so either there was a third wolf that wasn't yet visible or the bolt had fallen out. She hoped it was the latter.

The second wolf had been preparing to attack Grendel, but when Rev's bolt landed in its haunch, it turned and headed her way, clawing at the trunk of the tree. Pulling her legs up to her chest, she noticed that she was only about a foot away from the creature's sharp claws. Hopefully it didn't know how to jump.

From this position it was more difficult to find a good shot, but she pushed the terror down and waited for an opportunity. The arrow landed in the wolf's shoulder, but the animal paid no attention and continued its attack.

"We could have just walked on without bothering each other, but no…" Rev muttered to herself as she loaded another bolt, "you had to get all hungry for humans and attack us."

Before she could shoot again, the wolf let out a whimper and fell to the ground.

"Lots of wolves in the forests back home," Grendel said, wiping off his axe. "Smart ones knew not to bother us too much, but the dumb ones never quite learned. These ones probably haven't seen many humans travelling around these parts."

"I knew I kept you around for a reason," Rev joked. Before leaving the tree, she looked around the forest for any more wolves that might be hiding. There wasn't any movement that she could see, but then a flash of grey caught her eyes and she stared at the creature hidden in the forest. It stayed for a few seconds, but then moved away from them, heading further into the woods. Breathing a sigh of relief, she jumped to the ground.

"Let's hope that's all the excitement we have to deal with," she remarked as she collected her bolts from the fallen animal. Grendel nodded in agreement.

They continued along their intended path, luckily without coming across any more wolves or other creatures. After a while, the sky began to grow dark, and the two of them agreed that it would be best to find a place to settle for the night. If they'd been walking on a road they could have continued for a few hours more, but it wasn't safe to be trekking through the forest in the dark. They could twist an ankle or hurt themselves by not noticing uneven ground or fallen branches.

They found a place to settle down, but after putting their bedrolls on the ground and starting a fire, they realized that there was an anthill nearby and ants were crawling everywhere. They quickly picked everything up, giving it a good shake before packing it away, and buried the fire before moving on to another spot. It wasn't easy this far in the woods to find a good place to camp, but eventually they found another area that was big enough for the two of them to lie down and build a fire.

After using the fading light to check that there were no ants nearby, Grendel set about getting the fire going while Rev searched for the ideal spot to put her bedroll. It couldn't be too close to the firepit, otherwise she might wake up on fire, but she didn't want to put it too far away. Although the ground wasn't very soft or flat, after brushing away some rocks and branches, she created an area that would be comfortable enough for one night.

As darkness descended, they enjoyed a quiet meal around the firepit. Grendel wasn't the most verbose of the group, so there wasn't much talking, but Rev was okay with that. It was better than Corin incessantly asking questions – or, worse, wanting to ask questions but being too nervous to, and then acting weird until someone finally drew the words out of him.

After eating, Rev tossed some more wood on the fire, hoping that it'd be strong enough throughout the night to scare any curious animals away from them. Then Grendel and she settled down for a rest.

†

Rev could feel something brushing across her face, like strands of cotton at the edge of a blanket. Still half-asleep, she brought her hand up to swipe the cotton from her face, but instead of falling away, it stuck to her hand. Groaning, Rev put her hand down and tried to ignore the feeling, assuming it was part of a dream, but then she heard a strange skittering noise. There was something vaguely familiar about it, but she couldn't quite place it. The noise tugged at the back of her mind, urging her to remember something, but she wasn't sure what it was…

Another strand of cotton fell against her face, crossing over her nose and cheek, and she went completely still as her eyes flew open. The fire was still burning, providing enough light for her to see the dark shapes as they moved around the small camp. Her breath caught in her throat as she held herself still, knowing that freaking out and jumping up wouldn't help the situation Grendel and she were currently in.

Skittering around the camp were four of the largest spiders Rev had ever seen. They were about three feet high, with long thin legs and huge abdomens. Two of the spiders were moving around the camp, apparently keeping watch. On the other side of the fire, she could see one of the spiders standing over Grendel, laying long lines of silk over him, just like the one moving over her. It seemed to be early in the process, as she'd been able to move her hand, but how long would it be before they got serious about 'containing' their intended meal?

A shiver threatened to run down Rev's spine as she tried not to think about what might have happened if she hadn't woken up.

Grendel was still asleep, but his axe was close by. If she could wake him up without the spiders knowing then they could launch a sneak attack, but it wasn't very likely that she'd be able to wake him up, inform him of the situation, and prepare a plan without the spiders sensing anything. Any move she made would alert the creatures, and then they'd attack her. Just the thought of those sharp fangs digging into her skin made her want to cringe. She didn't like spiders much when they were a normal, small size, but these huge creatures made her skin want to crawl. She'd much rather have the wolves back.

Pushing her fear to the back of her mind, she tried to figure out what she could do. She'd been able to move her arm, so the spiders either didn't have paralyzing venom or didn't see the need to use it. She'd have to do something before Grendel and she were covered with too much webbing to move, and it made sense that the element of surprise would be the best option. Hopefully if she drew the attention of the spiders towards her, it'd give Grendel enough time to wake up, realize what was going on, and jump into action.

Rev closed her eyes and, although she didn't pray often, said a quick internal prayer to Dolos that her plan would work and she wouldn't end up as a meal for a hungry giant spider. Opening her eyes slightly, she steadied her breathing and waited until the spider crawling over her was near her feet before moving her hand up towards her cloak, which had been rolled into a pillow. There was a dagger lying next to it, which had been carefully placed before going to sleep. Grendel had suggested that she keep her weapons close and ready, in case they were attacked at night, and although she'd thought he was overreacting at the time, now she was glad to have followed his recommendation.

As her hand moved nearer to her weapon, she kept a close eye on the spiders. Their movements stayed the same as before, and it didn't appear that any of them had realized what she was doing.

Wishing that she had a larger weapon, Rev slowly curled her hand around the dagger and hoped that this would work. The spider crawled up towards her head, laying more strings across her face. Before it could turn, she grabbed the dagger and thrust it up into the spider's abdomen as deep as it could go. She slid down her bedroll, away from the spider, dragging the dagger through its abdomen as she went. As soon as she was far enough away, she raced towards the closest tree and climbed up, shouting curses at the spiders and trying to attract their attention.

The large creatures soon realized what she'd done and skittered her way – except for the one she'd attacked, which wasn't moving and was hopefully dead.

"Wake up! Giant spiders!" she yelled at Grendel as she dodged the spider legs reaching for her and scrambled further up the tree. She wished that she'd had enough time to grab her crossbow and bolts, but it was more important for her to make it up the tree and not get bitten. Swinging her dagger wildly, she knew that it wouldn't be much help against the giant creatures, but hopefully Grendel would wake up soon and realize what was going on.

One of the spiders reached for her with its unnaturally long and spindly legs, and Rev shrank away, hoping not to get cut by the sharp edges. She was still too close to the creatures, but the tree branches were too small and weak for her to climb any higher. The spiders didn't seem to be able to climb, which was fantastic news, but as long as she was within their reach she'd be in danger.

"Grendel!" she cried out, unable to tear her eyes off the immediate threat. "Spiders!"

She heard a kind of growling, but wasn't sure if it was Grendel or wolves. That would be great, she thought sarcastically, giant spiders and wolves attacking at once. She was never going into the forest again.

Suddenly the spindly legs fell back and she noticed that Grendel was standing near the bodies of three spiders at the base of the tree, his axe resting on the ground and his breathing heavy. He motioned with his head for her to come down, but she couldn't stop looking at the spiders.

"Can you chop them up a bit more?" she asked. "Just to be sure?"

Grendel picked at some of the silk that was still clinging to his clothing and nodded. As he went about his work, Rev watched from the tree, trying not to shiver at the thought of the spiders suddenly getting up and attacking them again.

When he was finished, she carefully made her way down the tree and over to her bedroll, which now had spider guts on it. For a moment she considered throwing it in the fire and buying a new one at the next town. Instead, she picked up her crossbow and bolts and clipped them onto her belt, vowing to never be without them again.

Grendel heaved a sigh and walked over to her.

"Is that all of them?" he asked.

Rev shrugged. "That's all that I could see." She looked into the darkness and felt a shiver run down her spine. What if the woods were full of these giant spiders? What if there were more out there, waiting for them to sleep so that they could ensnare and eat them? She'd thought the fire would keep them safe, but apparently it didn't work for all kinds of creatures.

"I think I'll stay up and keep watch," Grendel said, continuing to pick the silk off his clothes. His voice held only the slightest hint of fear, and Rev had a feeling that he was as unnerved by the incident as she was.

"I think I'll help," she replied, knowing full well that there was no way she'd be able to sleep anytime soon.

†

Neither of them slept for the rest of the night, not even nodding off for a second. No other creatures were seen, but they both jumped whenever they heard a sound in the woods, hands tightening around their respective weapons. As soon as the sun started to rise, they packed up and prepared to leave the camp. Rev used some of her water to clean the guts off her clothes, but didn't want to waste the rest on her bed-roll. Instead she cleaned it as best as she could using moss and leaves, deciding that it'd be better to have it on hand in case they were stuck in the woods for another night. Not that she'd be doing much sleeping if that were the case...

They rushed through the forest, eager to get as far away from the campsite as quickly as possible. Eventually exhaustion hit them and they had to slow down, their feet growing heavier with every step. Whereas their previous pace had been easy and relaxed, confident in their path, now they stumbled through the forest, weary and haunted. They paused and tensed at every sound, wondering what kind of danger might be waiting for them. Luckily they didn't come across any other creatures, but the mood remained grim. Neither spoke, choosing to stay quiet about their experiences. As the hours passed, the mountains grew larger in the distance, and soon the forest began to grow thinner.

When they reached the small clearing with the waterfall, Rev sighed in relief, thankful that this part of the experience was now over. Only after that did she realize that there was nobody else in the clearing and that Grendel and she were the first to arrive. Instead of jumping around or cheering, she looked over at Grendel.

"We don't tell them anything," she said seriously.

Grendel nodded solemnly. "Agreed."

The two of them sat down on the rocks around the waterfall, exhausted from their journey. Rev wondered if they had time for a nap, but before she could answer that question, two people emerged from the woods and made their way over. Rev tried her hardest to look relaxed.

"Hope we didn't keep you waiting too long," Aeris said as she approached.

Rev waved her hand dismissively. "We're taking time to enjoy the view. You know, relax before the big adventure."

"So I take it you two didn't come across any trouble on your path?" Corin asked.

†

To arrive at The Cave of Souls, continue forward.

Or you can go back to Aeris and Corin's Path
on Page 25.

THE CAVE OF SOULS

"Trouble?" Rev said, giving a laugh that sounded slightly strained. "We had a great time! How about you two?"

Corin looked over at Aeris.

"Nothing we couldn't handle," Aeris replied. "So, did you find the sigil?"

"Sigil?" Rev looked confused for a split second before the smile was back on her face. "Sorry, we were so busy taking in the sights that we forgot to look for the sigil." She jumped to her feet. "We might as well search for it now!"

Aeris noticed that Rev seemed tired and possibly a bit manic, but she decided not to ask any questions. After all, it was possible that Rev and Grendel had tried to find the sigil and failed, and Rev was merely covering it up.

The four of them set about searching the mountain-side for the mysterious carved symbol. They'd thought it would be easy to find, but after almost an hour of searching, they discovered it close to the ground, partially covered by the tall grass.

"If you think about it, that's a great place for a sigil," Rev said, keeping her tone light and cheerful. "There's no way anyone would happen to stumble upon that."

A few feet away from the sigil was a four-foot high opening in the rock. It was difficult to see how far it went into the mountain and whether it was a split in the rock or actually a cave, but it was close to where Dillen had told them the entrance would be.

"Guess this is it," Grendel said, sizing up the entrance.

Corin nodded, a look of determination crossing his face.

"Wait," Aeris quickly spoke up, raising her hand to stop them. "Before we go in, we need a plan. We don't know what kind of traps the wizard might have set up, and we'll never get any treasure if we end up teleported to another part of the world."

She'd expected a fight from the others, but they all paused and turned to her, waiting to hear what plan she had in mind. It threw her for a moment, causing her thoughts to scatter, but then she centred herself.

"We don't touch anything. And we don't go anywhere unless we've informed someone and they're okay with us going. We look first, talk about what we see, and figure out what to do next. Wizards can be tricky, so it's best to assume that everything is trapped."

Corin nodded in agreement, Grendel made a gruff sound while also nodding, and Rev gave a salute. Aeris wondered if this was what winning looked like.

She took the lead, which she knew was best because she'd be the most cautious. Corin was behind her, having conjured up a small globe of light to illuminate their path, with Rev behind him, and Grendel taking up the rear in case anything attacked from behind.

Ducking low to fit through the opening, Aeris followed the tunnel left, then right, and then breathed a sigh of relief as the ceiling suddenly rose, allowing her to stand at her full height. The tunnel wasn't very wide, but after following the strange, winding path for a long time, eventually she noticed a dim light at the end of the tunnel.

Stepping into a large, round room, she saw that the glow was emanating from four gems which had been placed into the wall, spread equidistant apart. They were all a different colour – purple, red, green, and blue. Corin's globe was brighter and illuminated the room easily, but there wasn't much else to look at. There were no obvious doors or pathways.

"Look around for any signs of hidden doorways or magical interference," she instructed the others, "but be careful."

They spread out and started searching. Rev's eyes scanned the room for any deceptions that might be hiding treasure from prying eyes, but when she couldn't find anything she decided to take a look at the gems in the wall, trying to figure out if they could be removed and how much they might be worth. Grendel begrudgingly moved about the room, glancing at the walls for any signs, but also keeping an eye on the room in case anything dangerous suddenly appeared.

Corin started near the door they'd come in through, carefully analyzing the wall. He knew that he was moving slower than the others, but he didn't want to risk missing something important. What if this large crack was part of a bigger message? What if this raised part of stone meant something?

Suddenly he noticed words carved into the wall, about two feet off the floor, not far from the entrance.

"I, um, I think I've found something," he said, crouching down a safe distance away from the wall. "It seems to be written in Mystic language."

The others moved over to him.

"Do you know what it says?" Aeris asked.

Corin screwed up his face. "It's some kind of poem about making a potion. *The water brings change, the grass brings health, the lilac brings power, and the blood brings life.*"

"If that's poetry, it's terrible," Grendel remarked.

"What does it mean?" Rev said, screwing up her face. "Do you think it's important? Or was this guy really into poetry?"

Aeris paused to think. "Change, health, power, life... Water, grass, lilac, blood..."

"Four!" Corin exclaimed. "There are four ingredients, four outcomes..."

"Four gems on the wall!" Rev finished excitedly.

"It must be a puzzle," Aeris said, walking over to the blue stone to take a closer look. There was something about the way the stone was set into the wall that made her wonder if it could be pressed. She looked at the other stones – purple, red, green. "Maybe we have to press all four stones in the order of the poem?"

Rev hurried over to the green stone. "Then let's get at it!"

"Wait!" Aeris paused. "It seems too simple."

Grendel shrugged. "Maybe it's not. I don't know any Mystic. Maybe he was hoping other people wouldn't."

"That's true," Rev said. "Or maybe he intentionally made it easy, because there are other precautions along the way. Dillen said something about skeletons and creatures, and there's nothing here. Maybe this is how we get to the next part of the cave – where all the treasure is hidden!"

Aeris didn't feel convinced, but she had to admit that their search hadn't discovered anything else. "As long as we're sure we're not missing anything else."

Leaning closer to the wall, Corin took a good look at the poem and the stone around it. "I don't think we're missing anything. If he wanted the gems pressed in reverse order, there would likely be something to indicate it."

Nodding, Aeris realized that it was their best chance and gave in, despite the uneasy feeling in her gut. "Well, let's all pick a gem and get ready."

As Corin headed over to the purple gem and Grendel to the red, Aeris went over the poem in her head. At least she was at the first gem, so if they did anything wrong she'd be the first to find out.

"Well, let's get the sequence started," Aeris said, mostly speaking to herself. Holding her sword at the ready, she braced herself for anything that her mind could imagine happening, while hoping that they weren't making a terrible mistake. Taking one last glance around the room, she noticed that Corin looked concerned and worried, Rev was smiling eagerly and likely thinking about treasure, and Grendel was standing ready for whatever might happen next.

Taking in a deep breath, Aeris recited, "*Water brings change,*" and pushed on the blue gem. She felt it slide into the wall and then stop. She turned to Rev, who was next, but suddenly the earth beneath her feet began to shake.

"What–" The word had barely come out of her mouth before a section of the floor beneath each person opened up and they all tumbled down.

†

To follow Corin into The Purple Chamber, continue forward

Or you can follow Rev into The Green Chamber on Page 67.

Or Grendel into The Red Chamber on Page 73.

Or Aeris into The Blue Chamber on Page 77.

Or you can skip over the rooms and enter The Wizard's Hallway on Page 85.

THE PURPLE CHAMBER

Corin landed on the ground in a heap. The fall hadn't been very far, probably only eight or ten feet, but he hadn't been expecting the floor to disappear beneath him and was unprepared for the landing. As he cautiously rose to his feet, he checked to make sure that nothing had been injured during his fall. Other than a sore bottom, he seemed to be fine – his arms and legs were working, and there were no broken bones or sprains.

There was a faint 'thud' above him, which he assumed was the trapdoor closing back up, and suddenly he realized that he had no idea where he'd landed.

"Aeris?" he called out, his voice weak and wavering with fear. There was no answer.

There was a faint purple glow lighting the room

from above, but it only illuminated a few feet around him, so he had no idea how big the room was or where the door might be. The floor seemed solid, but there was no guarantee that it didn't drop off suddenly at some point, leading into a massive deadly pit below. Holding his breath, he listened for any sounds, but the room was eerily silent.

Corin let out his breath in a sigh and tried to figure out what to do. He could remember seeing the others fall down, but it seemed that he was alone in this room, so they must be in other rooms. Did these rooms have doors? Would they be able to get out and find each other again? Or had they been dropped into pits where they'd starve to death, surrounded by the corpses of other adventurers who'd taken the same route?

Panic threatened to overtake him and he took a few deep breaths. He should at least try to find a way out before leaping to such terrible conclusions. It'd be embarrassing to give up only a few feet away from the exit.

Kneeling down, he carefully looked at the stone floor, searching for any traps or tricks. There were no stones that looked out of place or threads along the ground. Standing back up, he slowly turned around, but within the dim circle of purple light there was no way of knowing which direction was the right way.

A sudden thought hit him and he almost kicked himself for being so stupid. During the fall, he'd lost concentration on the ball of light and it had blinked out of existence. He'd been so panicked about the situation that he'd forgotten he could cast the spell again.

Suddenly the room was filled with glowing light. Corin let out a terrified gasp, his eyes growing wide with panic. Monstrous faces surrounded him on all sides, and he started firing lightening blasts and ice shards at them, hoping to keep them at bay.

After almost a minute of this, he realized that nothing was moving. He stopped casting spells and paused, taking a closer look at his surroundings. The monsters, although they had terribly wicked expressions on their faces, were still and unmoving. Some had arrows or pieces of metal sticking out of them. All of them were injured, and all were dead.

Feeling like a fool, Corin chided himself for using so many spells when he didn't have to. Normally Aeris and Grendel would attack, giving him time to figure out the best spell for the situation, but without them around he'd acted in panic.

Other than his recent battles with the group, he hadn't been in many fights. When he'd started learning magic, his favourite spells were ones that protected him or were helpful. In fact, all of his attack spells had been learned so that he could vanquish the evil wizard Grimgrax and avenge his mentor, Wileth.

He thought back to the evil wizard that had designed this cave. How many magic users became evil? If he decided to learn more spells, would he eventually turn down the dark path and stop caring about other people? After all, without Wileth around, he had nobody else to keep him in check. Well, nobody but Aeris, Rev, and Grendel. Although he wasn't certain about the last two, he knew that Aeris would have no trouble telling him if he was doing questionable things. But Aeris didn't seem to want to stay with the group. He could see the exasperation on her face at times, and wondered how long it would be before she left them. As much as Corin was starting to feel affection for this strange group of people, he knew that Aeris was the only reason he was still with them. If she left, would she allow him to tag along, or would she rather be alone?

Pulling his mind from such thoughts, he focused on the task at hand – trying to find a way to escape this room. He began exploring the walls, looking for any kind of indication that there might be a door or a passage, while keeping a safe distance from the dead monsters, just in case they became reanimated.

Finally, he found an area of the floor that seemed to have scrapes on it, arcing away from the wall. Bringing the globe of light closer, he examined the stones around that area, searching for one that didn't look the same as the others. He was careful to take his time and look extra hard, but when he stumbled upon a stone about waist high, he noticed how obviously different it was. Apparently this wizard didn't go for subtlety.

Double-checking that the floor was solid beneath him and that there were no indications it might split open again, he braced himself and pressed the stone.

†

To follow Rev into The Green Chamber,
continue forward.

Or follow Grendel into The Red Chamber on Page 73.

Or Aeris into The Blue Chamber on Page 77.

Or you can skip over the rooms and enter
The Wizard's Hallway on Page 85.

THE GREEN CHAMBER

Rev managed to land in a low crouch, hands and feet on the floor, joints bent to better absorb the shock. She didn't much like falling, but she'd jumped from many high buildings in the past. Heck, she'd willingly jumped from windows higher than that fall had been, just to feel a thrill.

A sound made her look up and she noticed that the hole in the ceiling was closing up. Not that she could have reached it, but maybe there was a rope or ladder or something around here... Of course, none of that would help unless there was a way to open the trap-door again.

The room had a green glow to it, but there were still plenty of shadows. It was larger than she'd expect-ed, which hopefully meant that there was a way out. After all, why would the wizard bother wasting so much space on a room someone was never meant to leave?

She called out for the others, but there was no reply. She was all alone.

A strange, familiar noise sounded behind her. Rev felt her blood run cold as her mind recognized the skittering sound, and a terrified gasp escaping her lips as the memory of last night came forth. She quickly had a dagger in each hand, turning around to face the sound.

Her heart started beating faster and her eyes darted from side to side, trying to see the monsters skittering around the room. After not finding anything, her eyes started moving up the wall and soon she saw it. It wasn't as big as the spiders that had attacked Grendel and her at the camp, but it was about two feet tall and its legs were unnaturally long.

"Why does it have to be spiders?" she whimpered, thankful that none of the others were around to hear the fear in her voice. That thanks quickly turned into regret as she realized that she was all alone. She wasn't the most skilled fighter in the group, and if it hadn't been for Grendel's intervention she'd probably have been sliced and diced by a spider leg back in the woods. If Grendel or Aeris were here, they'd be able to take care of this problem, and she could safely hide behind them,but they weren't.

Rev held her breath and kept her eyes on the spider as she slowly moved her hand to her side. It was too high for her to stab, so she'd need her crossbow to deal with it. All she needed to do was switch weapons without the creature moving and then she'd—

The spider suddenly dropped, and she shrieked.

Forgetting about the crossbow, she held both daggers in front of her. The spider dropped to the floor and rushed towards her, it's long legs skittering along the stones. Rev could see the green light glinting off its sharp fangs and she tightened her grip on the daggers.

It leapt towards her, and she frantically sliced the air with her daggers, managing to catch the spider with one of them, and causing it to retreat to the shadows. She almost regretted losing sight of it, but at least it wasn't close to her anymore. Maybe she could hold it off until someone else found her and was able to take care of it, but that would depend on someone being able to find her. Besides, she'd have to stay in here with the spider until that happened, and any amount of time longer than one second was too long to spend in this room.

She quickly traded the dagger in her right hand for the crossbow, her eyes darting around the room, watching for any movement. Holding her breath, she listened for any sound that might indicate its location. There were noises in front of her as the spider started to climb up the wall, moving towards the ceiling. She wasn't sure how a spider could climb a stone wall, unless it was covered in webs. A shiver ran along her spine as that mental image appeared, but it was interrupted by the sound of something behind her.

Rev's heart sank. There were two of them.

She started to move away from the sounds, but then remembered the image of walls covered in cobwebs and the feel of those webs across her face. Stopping suddenly, she tried to think of everything in her inventory. She needed to see the room better, but Corin wasn't here with his magic light and she didn't have a lantern. She had flint and steel, but that wouldn't be much help without something to catch on fire, and it would take too long to get a good flame.

Then she remembered the sunsticks. She'd bought them a while ago, before meeting up with the group, but with Corin's ability to conjure light she hadn't needed them. They were expensive, and she hated having to use one of them in a room that she'd hope-fully be leaving very soon, but desperate times...

Keeping an ear out for the spiders, she slowly took off her backpack and lowered it to the floor. Reluct-antly putting away the dagger in her left hand, she rummaged through her pack for one of the sunsticks. She wasn't sure how many she had left from the original five she'd purchased, but there had to be at least one.

A noise to her left made her freeze, and she held up the crossbow, pointing it towards the noise, but she couldn't see anything in the darkness. She began rummaging again, finally closing her fingers around a thin glass tube. Pulling it free, she held it close to her face and whispered a few words to activate the magic within.

A bright yellow light began to glow from inside the tube, and soon the room was illuminated in light. Rev felt her heart sink. Along the walls, waiting among the multitude of woven webs, were six spiders.

Letting out a shriek, Rev dropped the tube and started firing her crossbow, reloading faster than she'd ever reloaded before. The sudden light had stunned the spiders, and she was able to take down four of them before any started moving. The fifth spider managed to dodge her bolt, skittering along the wall, and she quickly reloaded. She managed to hit it with the second shot, stopping it, but when she looked for the sixth spider, it wasn't in sight.

A sharp pain in her side told her where the spider was. Stumbling forward, she tried to turn around and aim her crossbow, but tripped up in her own feet and fell to the ground. The spider raised its front leg for another stab, and she wasn't able to get out of the way fast enough. The sharp point scraped along her leg, tearing through her pants and skin. Letting out another cry, Rev fired the crossbow, but the shot was wild and missed entirely. The spider raised its leg again and she rolled out of the way, fumbling for another bolt. As she tried to reload, the spider attacked again, and she decided that it was more important to reload than dodge. The spider's leg sliced along her calf and pain seared through her, but she managed to get the bolt loaded and aimed it at the spider's face. One shot took it down.

Rev stayed on the floor, breathing hard, searching around the room for more spiders, but they seemed to all be dead. Ignoring the pain in her leg and side, she took the time to gather her sanity and slow her heart-rate. After a few minutes she was convinced that there was no more danger, and made her way over to her pack. Digging through it, she found some bandages and started tending to the cuts on her leg and side. Although she hadn't been bitten, she made a mental note to watch for any signs that she'd been poisoned.

When her wounds had been tended to, she stayed on the floor for a few more seconds, trying to pull herself together. She'd never felt so much fear and panic before, and even though she knew she was now safe, those feelings hadn't fully subsided.

From where she sat, she tried to figure out where the exit was, which wasn't difficult thanks to the bright light. The outline in the stone was quite obvious when compared to the rest of the room, and thankfully it wasn't covered in webs.

Taking a deep breath, she pulled herself to her feet and gathered her things. She managed to take back a few bolts from the spiders that had fallen to the floor, but some were tangled high up in the webs, so she ignored those. Then she picked up the sunstick, thankful that the glass was thick enough not to have shattered on the ground when she'd dropped it. Her left hand gripped it tightly, and she hoped that it would last long enough for her to get out of this godforsaken room.

Going over to the door, she tried to push it open, but it wouldn't budge. Sighing, she figured that there must be some kind of trick to it. Looking around, she spied one brick that was different than all the others. Taking a deep breath, she prayed that there were no more spiders behind this door and pressed the brick, causing the door to swing open.

†

To follow Grendel into The Red Chamber,
continue forward.

Or follow Aeris into The Blue Chamber on Page 77.

Or Corin into The Purple Chamber on Page 61.

Or you can skip over the rooms and enter
The Wizard's Hallway on Page 85.

THE RED CHAMBER

Grendel landed with a 'thud', hitting the ground hard. The impact was rough, but he didn't feel any injury from it. He even managed to keep hold of his axe.

Standing up, he held his axe ready, prepared to fight anything that came his way. But nothing came. He waited, peering into the red-hued darkness, but nothing moved in the shadows or made a sudden rush towards him. After a few minutes, Grendel eventually lowered his axe, confused.

He wondered if maybe the creatures in this room had been killed by previous travellers. Or maybe the wizard had assumed nobody would press the red gem and didn't bother putting anything in the room.

Sighing, he looked around, trying to figure out which way to go, but the entire room looked the same.

The floor was stone, the walls were stone, and the ceiling was too high up for him to get a good look at, but it was probably also stone. The hole he'd fallen through had closed up, leaving him with only the strange red hue lighting the area. Scouring the room, he tried to figure out where the light was coming from, but had no idea.

Figuring that he might as well get on with it, Grendel started walking towards a random wall. The room was square and there were no distinguishing features on any of them, so he hoped that getting closer would reveal some kind of way to get the heck out of here. However, on his fourth step he felt something depress under his foot and instantly stopped. Had he heard a 'click' or had he imagined it? Was this some kind or trap or was the stone merely loose?

He stood still for a while, not sure what to do next. The best course of action would be to try to go back the way he'd come, but could he do that without triggering the trap? What kind of trap could it be? And was there even a trap to worry about? It was possible that it had gone defunct over time and wouldn't work, but he knew it was better to be safe than sorry and not end up with an arrow in the knee.

Taking in a deep breath, Grendel put his other foot as far back as possible while still maintaining his balance. Leaning back, he let out a breath and quickly stepped back, taking his foot off the depressed stone. A thin bolt whizzed through the air, passing through the empty space where his torso had been, and he breathed a sigh of relief.

The relief didn't last long, however, as he came to the realization that not only was this room booby-trapped, but the traps were all still working. He couldn't help grumbling under his breath. Traps were supposed to be Rev's problem, not his. It was almost enough to make him want to sit down on the floor and wait for someone else to find him and deal with it. Unfortunately, he suspected that everyone else was dealing with some kind of trap of their own, and – depending on what those traps were – they might be stuck for hours or days. If he wanted to get out of this room, he'd have to figure out it himself.

As much as it pained him, Grendel started making his way towards the wall, moving slowly and carefully. He briefly entertained the idea of running forward at full speed, hoping that he'd be fast enough to avoid the bolts, but without Aeris nearby to heal him, he knew that it'd be foolish to risk getting injured. Instead, he took it one painstakingly slow step at a time, searching for safe stones to step on.

A few times he almost fell, and the one time he did stumble, he managed to land on a safe area. Eventually he was able to recognize a pattern in the dangerous stones, so he picked up his speed, eager to get the heck out of this room.

By the time he made his way to the wall, he still hadn't heard anyone else's voice or seen another person. He hoped that the others were still alive. Searching the door, he found one stone that looked like a trigger, but he wasn't sure if it'd open the door or launch a trap. It would make sense if it was the door, because why would someone bother setting up traps if they didn't block the intruder's way out? Shrugging to himself, he pushed the stone. He'd wasted enough time in this stupid room already.

After a few seconds, a section of the wall started to move inward, revealing the way out.

†

To follow Aeris into The Blue Chamber,
continue forward.

Or follow Corin into The Purple Chamber on Page 61.

Or Rev into The Green Chamber on Page 67.

Or you can skip over the rooms and enter
The Wizard's Hallway on Page 85.

THE BLUE CHAMBER

Aeris landed in a low crouch, trying to absorb the shock from the landing throughout her whole body. She noticed a blue glow illuminating the room, but there was no time for her to take in anything else as she detected an animated skeleton making its way towards her, its axe raised high in the air.

She quickly brought her sword up and around as she rose to her feet, slicing the skeleton through the spine. As the skeleton clattered to the floor, she noticed two more behind it – one with a longsword and the other with a warhammer. It took a few hits to dispatch the one with the sword, her first and second attacks only managed to break ribs before she finally guided her sword to its spine, severing it with one quick strike.

Her reward was a hit to the left arm with the

warhammer by the remaining skeleton. Gritting her teeth, she ignored the pain in her arm and parried the next attack with her sword. This skeleton put up a good fight, but she soon cut it in half.

Breathing heavily, she glanced around the room, ready for more enemies to appear, but there was no more movement or sound. She assumed that the others had fallen elsewhere, considering how far away they'd been in the cave, and how she hadn't heard any yells for help.

Moving over to the nearest wall, she began searching for signs of a door or a way out of the room, but there was nothing to be found. As she moved onto the next wall, she heard a strange clicking sound behind her and turned around. Her eyes scanned the walls and ceiling, wondering what strange creature could be hiding in the shadows, but then she noticed movement on the floor. The skeleton bones were rattling, and if she didn't know any better, she'd say that they were starting to move...

"Oh no!" Aeris quickly turned to the wall and searched frantically for the door. If she was right, then the enchantment that animated those skeletons could also bring them back together. If she didn't find the door soon, she'd have to fight them again and again and again...

Her eyes widened as she spotted an odd stone and she quickly pressed it, not stopping to think of the possible consequences. A part of the wall started to swing towards her and she quickly slipped through, ending up in a long hallway. Facing the door, she kept her sword ready, but then the door closed, shutting the skeletons inside.

Letting out a sigh of relief, Aeris let her sword drop and took a moment get her heartbeat back under control. Then she looked around the hallway, wondering what to do next.

To one side was a dead end, while the other went on, disappearing around a bend. She was the only one in the hallway. The fight with the skeletons had turned her around and made her lose her bearings, so she had no idea where the others might be located. She could remember watching them fall, so they must be in other rooms, but where would those be? Were there more doors along this hallway or were there other hallways connected to this one? She looked along the walls but there were no strange stones in the walls or marks on the floor, or anything else that might indicate a hidden door nearby. Her own door seemed to have vanished into the stone after closing, so maybe the other doors were equally as well hidden. Or maybe they were somewhere else.

Aeris wasn't sure what to do, but she knew that she wouldn't be able to help anyone if she couldn't find them. Perhaps there was a lever somewhere that controlled the doors, and if she found it she could let everyone else out.

Taking in a deep breath, she walked confidently down the hallway, keeping an eye out for any levers or odd stones, and an ear out for any cries for help. The hallway twisted and turned, but there were no other rooms or signs of secret passageways. She had walked far enough that she was beginning to regret her decision to leave that part of the hallway, but then she turned a corner and noticed a light up ahead.

Increasing her speed, Aeris made her way towards

the light, and soon she found herself in a large room with small white glowing crystals set into the wall. There were a few objects scattered on the floor – old armour, weapons, a few bags that were probably filled with coins – but at the back of the room was a pedestal with a large white gem in the middle, glowing weakly. Aeris could barely take her eyes off the gem, and she found herself unconsciously walking towards it.

"Greetings traveller," a melodic voice resonated throughout the room.

"Hel... Hello," Aeris said, wondering if the voice was coming from the crystal. "Are you the young woman who was trapped in the crystal?"

"Yes," the voice answered. "I've been waiting for so long to be set free."

Aeris looked around the pedestal, searching for some kind of button or writing. In the back of her mind she wondered if she should try to free the others first, but then she realized that they'd only get in the way. As soon as this soul was saved, she'd find a way to free them. Heck, maybe the soul would know how to get them out.

"How do I free you?" she asked. "Is there a spell?"

"There is no spell. There is only one way that my freedom can be achieved, and it is too much for me to ask of you." The voice took on a melancholy tone.

"What is the way?" Aeris asked. "I am a paladin and I am sworn to protect others. If I can release you from your prison, then I will."

"The spell I am under is a terrible one. It demands that a sacrifice be given in exchange for my freedom. But I cannot ask that of anyone."

Aeris paused. "What kind of sacrifice?"

"It demands that a life be taken. Only then, through the ultimate sacrifice that a person can give, will my soul be released from this terrible prison. Once I am free, I will be able to restore that life back again, but the act required is too much to ask. I am afraid that I must remain in this crystal forever, never to feel the sun on my face or the wind in my hair."

As much as Aeris felt sad for the soul trapped inside the crystal, the request sent a shiver down her spine. Take her own life? The spirit had said that it would be able to bring her back after, but Aeris wasn't sure if she'd be able to do something so drastic.

"Is there another way?" she asked.

"There is not," the voice said mournfully. "I understand if you would like to leave me here all alone, like many others have done. It has been so long since I have talked to another person, let alone dreamed of being rescued. But I will understand if you choose to leave."

The words set about a war inside of Aeris. She desperately wanted to help this soul – after all, nobody should be forced to live their life trapped inside a crystal. But the cost was so high. What if the spirit had been weakened and was unable to restore her life? What if something went wrong? What if the sacrifice wasn't considered good enough?

"Are you sure there is no other sacrifice that would work?" Aeris said, trying to keep the discomfort out of her voice. "What exactly did the wizard say to you? Was it 'the ultimate sacrifice' or 'only death can set you free'?"

"There is no other way," the voice replied. "It is death or nothing."

Aeris began to pace around the room. "But what if there's some kind of trick in it? What if I kill myself and nothing happens, and then you're still trapped and I'm dead?"

"It is death or nothing," the voice repeated firmly. "Only death can set me free."

Aeris wondered if she'd said the wrong thing. Perhaps she shouldn't be trying to negotiate with a soul that had been trapped in a crystal. Who knows how long it had been since it was placed here... She tried to imagine what it would be like if she had been imprisoned in a crystal and stuck in a cave, and if she'd waited so long for someone else to appear, only to start asking banal questions.

It was her duty to help. And it would only be temporary, after all. Aeris took in a deep breath. Her job was to be brave and bold, and to trust the gods that she would be protected.

Lifting her sword, she placed it against her throat. As she did so, she noticed that the crystal had started to glow brighter. Aeris began to apply pressure, but as the sharp edge of her sword began to bite into her skin, she stopped. She lowered the sword.

"I'm sorry," Aeris said, her voice filled with regret. "I want to help, but I cannot do this. There has to be another way."

The crystal began to pulse with energy. Aeris watched as the brilliant white light turned dark purple.

"If you cannot kill yourself, then I shall have to do it for you!"

The voice that came from the crystal was dark and sinister, and nothing like before. Aeris' eyes widened in confusion as a jolt of energy burst from the crystal and struck her. Letting out a yell as the energy pierced her chest, she fell to her knees, her sword falling from her hand. It felt as if she was paralyzed. She was unable to do anything but watch as her energy was slowly sucked out of her and into the crystal.

†

To enter The Wizard's Hallway,
continue forward.

Or you can go back to Corin in
The Purple Chamber on Page 61.

Or Rev into The Green Chamber on Page 67.

Or Grendel in the Red Chamber on Page 73.

THE WIZARD'S HALLWAY

Rev hurried through the door, brushing the cobwebs off her clothing. She had never been so happy to be out of a room in her life. The Cave of Souls? More like the Cave of Spiders. Ugh. Hopefully the reward would be worth the reoccurring nightmares she'd have from this ordeal.

"Rev?"

She turned and noticed Corin standing a few feet away, his ball of light hovering just above his head. He was a little twitchy, but didn't seem any worse for wear.

"How long have you been there?" she asked him.

"Just a few seconds. I came out around there," he pointed at the wall in front of him. "I tried looking for other doors, but couldn't even find my own. I wasn't sure what to do, so I stuck around in case anyone else came out."

Rev looked at the wall and, sure enough, she couldn't even make out the lines of her own door. Squinting, she brought her sunstick closer to the wall and tried to find any sign that a door might be carved in it. Finally, she noticed that one line of the grouting was a tiny bit higher than the rest, and the stones that interfered with the line of grouting were slightly rougher than the others. Stepping back, she looked at the long hallway the two of them were standing in. If she had to closely examine every single line of grouting to find the other doors, they'd be here for ages.

"I found some kind of clue, but I can't find a trigger for opening the doors," she said. She started pushing some stones that she assumed lined up with the trigger on the other side, but nothing happened. "I guess we'll have to wait for the others to get out on their own."

Corin shrugged and nodded. "I guess."

They stood silently in the hallway, each hoping that Aeris and Grendel would soon appear.

"So, what was your room like?" Rev asked, once the silence finally got the best of her.

His face screwed up into a pained look as he recalled the memory. "There were wolves and a few bodies, but everything was dead."

"Lucky," she muttered enviously. Why couldn't she have dropped into the room where everything was already dead?

"Why? What was your room like?" he asked.

Pausing, she let out a breath. "Spiders. Don't really want to talk about it."

Before Corin could say anything else, a part of the

wall opened and Grendel stumbled into the hallway.

"Finally," he huffed, standing upright. "That room was the worst."

Rev raised an eyebrow.

"What was in there?" Corin asked.

"Buncha traps." He frowned. "Nothing to fight at all. I hated it."

Rev wanted to argue that her room was the worst, but she kept her mouth shut. The sooner she could forget about all of this, the better.

"Well, that's three of us," Corin said, trying to put a bit of optimism into the current situation. "We just need Aeris now."

"Kinda figured she'd be the first one out," Grendel remarked, "seeing as how she's all high and mighty about being a paladin."

"Maybe the room she ended up in had a bunch of things to fight," Corin said. Although he tried to sound nonchalant, he was worried that Aeris hadn't arrived yet. She was quite strong and resourceful, so surely she'd be able to escape soon. But what would they do if a lot of time passed and she didn't show up? How long should they wait for her?

Rev looked around the hallway, wishing she had some way of telling how much time had passed since they'd entered the cave. It couldn't have been a lot, but down in these dimly lit rooms, how could anyone tell?

The three of them stood silently, waiting. Rev played with her sunstick, twirling it around; Grendel examined his axe for any injuries it may have received over the past few days; and Corin crossed his arms and tried not to think of what terrible thing Aeris might be fighting all alone.

Suddenly the silence was broken by a distant yell further down the hallway, and the three of them jumped to attention.

"Let's go!" Grendel said, hefting his axe.

"But Aeris..." Corin countered.

"That might have been her," Rev replied, hurrying down the hallway.

The three of them raced towards the yell, rushing down the long, twisting path. When they reached the end, they all froze at the sight ahead of them.

Aeris was kneeling on the ground, hunched over and in pain. In front of her was a stone pedestal with a large dark purple crystal on top. A bright bolt of energy was flowing between Aeris and the crystal.

Grendel's mouth dropped open as he took in the scene. "What the...?"

Corin's eyes widened and he rushed over to Aeris' side, calling up his shield and trying to move it between Aeris and the crystal. As it met with the energy bolt, he could feel resistance, but after some effort and pushing he could sense that it was helping to block some of the energy coming from the crystal.

Rev quickly took in the scene. They were here to rescue a soul trapped in a crystal, but this didn't look like a rescue mission – the crystal seemed to be hurting Aeris. Around the room, she could see abandoned armour and weapons in piles on the floor, so maybe this wasn't the first time the crystal had tried to kill an adventurer.

"I think the crystal's evil," she cried out.

Hearing Rev's words, Grendel lifted his axe and rushed for the crystal. It offered no resistance as he approached, continuing to focus its energies on Aeris.

Bringing the axe up high, he swung with all his might. There was a burst of light as the two connected and a loud crack formed in the crystal. The bolt of energy wavered as the crystal began to pulse and spark. Grendel quickly hefted his axe again, slamming it into the crystal, which shattered into pieces, falling to the ground and going dark.

The four of them stared at the pieces in shock, unsure what to do.

"What the hell was that?" Grendel asked, still holding his axe ready.

"That was one heck of an evil crystal," Rev said.

"You're right," Aeris replied, her voice tired and full of pain. She tried to stand up, but her strength wasn't quite there yet, so Corin grabbed her arm and helped her to her feet. "It wanted me to kill myself to set it free. When I refused, it attacked me."

"Wow," Rev gave a low whistle. She looked at the piles of stuff on the floor. "That definitely explains all the stuff here. If they didn't off themselves, the crystal probably vaporized them."

She started to move towards the nearest pile, but something in the corner of her eye caught her attention and she froze in place. Grendel saw this and took a step forward, preparing to strike, but Aeris quickly called out.

"Wait!" Aeris said. She looked over at the strange apparition that had suddenly appeared. It was white and transparent enough for her to make out the stone wall behind it. Aeris stepped towards the spirit, inadvertently bringing Corin with her, who was still helping her stand but also gripping her arm in fear.

"Are you the true spirit?" Aeris asked cautiously.

The ghost shook its head. "I am not the spirit of the crystal. It was destroyed when the crystal was destroyed. But I was trapped inside with it."

Suddenly other ghosts appeared throughout the room. Soon there were ten other spirits with them. They all looked like adventurers, with various armour or robes, but all stood either alone or in pairs.

"We were all killed and trapped in the crystal," the first ghost said. "No one could move onto the other side while the evil spirit lived. But now we are free."

Another ghost brought its hand up and touched its chin, before lowering the hand towards the four adventurers in a move of thanks. Then the ghosts all began to shimmer and fade, until the group were the only ones left in the room.

Corin let out a long breath. "Well, that wasn't quite what we were expecting, but I guess we managed to do some good. Right?"

Grendel lowered his axe. "I guess. It'd probably be terrible gettin' stuck in a crystal for all eternity."

"It's too bad the part about the treasure was just as fictional as the story about the trapped spirit," Rev sighed. She walked over to the nearest pile and started rummaging through it. "Might as well see if there's anything we can take. They won't need it where they're going."

THE PATH OUT

After looking through the armour and weapons left behind, the group managed to find some bags of coins and gems, and a few useful items. While it wasn't quite the haul they'd been expecting, it was better than nothing, and some of the weapons left behind were still in good enough shape to be sold or traded. Rev pocketed a short sword for herself, having realized that it'd be a good idea to have a weapon longer than a dagger, and she managed to find a few bolts. Grendel found a pair of leather bracers that were still in good shape, but other than taking some coin, he didn't grab anything else. He did offer to carry some of the weapons so that they could trade them at the next town. Aeris also offered to carry some weapons, after taking a few coins and a small silver necklace; while Corin decided to take nothing but gems, coins, and a few spell ingredients.

With the danger removed, the group decided to have a short rest. Aeris filled them in on how she'd come to the room without them, explaining how she honestly thought that she'd find them at the end of the hallway. Despite her words, Corin could tell that she felt bashful about approaching the gem without them, and as the rest of the group began to talk of their own escapes, she fell silent and didn't say anything else.

Rev didn't want to talk about her room, other than mentioning spiders, while Grendel grimaced as he recounted all the traps he'd had to avoid and how annoying the whole ordeal had been. Corin seemed to be the lucky one, having ended up in a room where everything was already dead. He couldn't help omitting the part where he'd panicked and wasted a bunch of spells.

After the details of the other rooms had been divulged, they tried to figure out how the story of the wizard had come about. Perhaps the evil soul in the crystal had a friend who'd spread that story, thinking it'd be a great way to attract adventurers to the cave. Or maybe there had been a trapped spirit and it had been released, but then this evil spirit somehow became trapped inside the crystal. A lot of hypothesis flew around, but Aeris said little and spent most of her time staring at the silver chain she had taken.

Once they had all rested, they realized that it was time to find a way out of the cave. Rising reluctantly to their feet, they began searching the room, looking for an exit. Using her sunstick, Rev managed to find a small door behind the pedestal, which open into another hallway. They all ducked through the door and made their way down the hall; Aeris, then Corin, Rev, and Grendel. The hallway soon led to a steep staircase made of stone, and the group made their way up, up, up, until finally the floor levelled out again.

"Are we there yet?" Grendel muttered.

Rev and Corin stifled a laugh, and Aeris gave a small smile as she shook her head.

The sunstick darkened soon after, so Corin called up his light to lead the way. A few feet later they reached another wall, and after a quick search by Rev and the push of a stone, a door opened in the wall and the four of them stumbled out into the fresh, night air.

"Well that was one heck of an adventure," Rev remarked, taking in a deep breath of cool air. It felt wonderful after breathing the stale air inside the cave. "I wonder if anyone will believe us."

Grendel let out a laugh. "I'm still not sure I believe what happened, and I was there."

"Should we camp here for the night or search for an inn?" Corin asked as he brushed dirt from his robes.

Grendel and Rev exchanged a look. As much as the two of them wanted to run for the nearest inn, they needed to play it cool and not let on how terrible their overnight experience in the forest had been.

Aeris looked up in the sky, trying to locate the moon. It hadn't yet climbed over the mountains, so she figured that it wasn't too far into the night. Although she felt weary, she wasn't tired.

"The town's not too far away," she said. "I think we've all earned a good sleep and a nice meal." She raised her eyebrows to the others. "What do we think?"

Rev nodded emphatically. "A hot meal and bed

sound wonderful."

Grendel and Corin also agreed, and the group set off for the trail to town, Corin's light leading the way.

As they walked, Aeris fell behind, lost in thought. Before this journey she'd been ready to walk away from the group, thinking that they'd been holding her back, but now she realized that this wasn't the case. Sure, they could be insufferable at times, but if they hadn't been in that cave with her, her soul would be trapped in a crystal right now.

They'd all gone on this adventure for selfish reasons, but had managed to do a lot of good. All of those souls would still be trapped if they hadn't come along; and if the crystal hadn't been destroyed then many more people could have died. She thought about the silver chain she'd taken from the cave. Normally she didn't care too much for jewelry, but she'd wanted to keep this one to remind her of this adventure. A person could be strong, but a group could be stronger.

Smiling to herself, she decided that it was time to put her ego aside and see just how much good this group could do.

"I just got it!" Rev exclaimed, coming to a sudden stop and causing Grendel to almost crash into her. "That's why it was called the Cave of Souls! Because there were all those other souls trapped inside the crystal!" She looked around at the others, sufficiently pleased with herself.

Corin paused to ponder what she'd said. "That makes sense. I think you're right."

Aeris exchanged a look with Grendel, who hadn't thought much about the name either way, and he shrugged at her. She shrugged back, and then congratulated Rev on finally solving the mystery of the cave's name.

ABOUT THE AUTHOR

(Photo by Morgana Kay)

Ali is the author of sci-fi/fantasy novels *The Six Elemental* and *The Fifth Queen*, and the short story collection *The Lightbulb Forest*. Numerous short stories of hers have appeared in Engen Book's 'From the Rock' series.

She spends most of her time scribbling stories and ideas in notebooks, and is rarely found without paper and pen. She is an avid traveller, foodie, and fan of the Oxford comma.

Currently she lives in Halifax with her computer and four swords, surrounded by over-flowing book-shelves and too many ideas.

HEED THE CALL

After a heated fight at sea between twins Ben and Alex, Ben vanishes from their boat without a sound or even a ripple in the water. Unwavering in his dedication to find his brother, Alex begins the adventure of a lifetime armed only with the help of a local girl named Meg and his own mysterious musical abilities... the key to which, and to the mysteries that surround him, may be tied to the alluring song of the dangerous girl he finds among the ocean's frothing waves.

"A mysterious figure in the ocean, a suspicious loss in the waves, a riveting treasure hunt, and surprise after surprise, how could anyone not want to read this novel?"
~Alice Kuipers, author of *Life on the Refrigerator Door*

"Loved this book and can't wait for the next one."
~Helen Escott, bestselling author of *Operation: Wormwood*

"It's been a while since I've read an entire book in one day, but...Whenever I tried to put it down, it would call out to me, luring me back like a siren's song."
~Ali House, author of *The Six Elemental & The Fifth Queen*

The early years of **Xander Drew** as he struggles with the evils of his small rural hometown of Coral Beach, Maine. Cursed with the heart of the Womb and the gift of seeing the world around him for what it really is, Xander must learn hard lessons about the nature of humanity to traverse the minefield of criminals, gangs, and abusers that stand between him and ultimate happiness

-- but most of all that **sometimes it takes a monster, to catch a monster.**

"THE WRITING OF ITS GENERATION- - VISUAL, TO-THE-POINT AND IN-THE-MOMENT."
- The Northeast Avalon Times

The Coral Beach Casefiles series by Matthew LeDrew:
Book One: Black Womb (February 2019)
Book Two: Transformations in Pain (March 2019)
Book Three: Smoke and Mirrors (April 2019)
Book Four: Roulette (May 2019)
Book Five: Ghosts of the Past (June 2019)
Book Six: Ignorance is Bliss (July 2019)
Book Seven: Becoming (August 2019)
Book Eight: Inner Child (September 2019)
Book Nine: Gang War (October 2019)
Book Ten: Chains (November 2019)
Epilogue: The Long Road (December 2019)

For more information, please visit
www.engenbooks.com